Rosie's Roses

by Pamela Duncan Edwards • illustrated by Henry Cole

HarperCollins Publishers

Also by Pamela Duncan Edwards and Henry Cole

FOUR FAMISHED FOXES AND FOSDYKE

SOME SMUG SLUG

LIVINGSTONE MOUSE

BAREFOOT: *ESCAPE ON THE UNDERGROUND RAILROAD*

THE WORRYWARTS

ROAR! *A NOISY COUNTING BOOK*

CLARA CATERPILLAR

WAKE~UP KISSES

Library of Congress Cataloging-in-Publication Data
Edwards, Pamela Duncan.
    Rosie's roses / by Pamela Duncan Edwards ; illustrated by
Henry Cole.— 1st ed.
            p.   cm.
    Summary: Rosie has four roses for her aunt's birthday, but after
four animals "borrow" one, her gift is reduced to a rainbow ribbon.
    ISBN 0-06-028997-X — ISBN 0-06-028998-8 (lib. bdg.)
    [1. Roses—Fiction. 2. Aunts—Fiction. 3. Gifts—Fiction.] I. Cole,
Henry, ill. II. Title.
PZ7.E26365 Ro 2003   2002008875
[E]—dc21

Typography by Elynn Cohen   1 2 3 4 5 6 7 8 9 10 ❖
First Edition

For our dear friends Kath and Ru Allen
and their super children and grandchildren, with love
—P.D.E.

To Pam
—H.C.

There's an *R* hidden in every picture in this book.
Can you find them all?

It was Aunt Ruth's birthday. Rosie had four roses for Aunt Ruth's present.

"Carry your roses carefully," warned her big brother, Robert, as he tied a rainbow ribbon around them.

Rosie and Robert hadn't rambled far when Rosie frowned.

"This is weird," she said. "My orange rose has disappeared."

"Perhaps you dropped your rose near that rotted log," said Robert. "I'm sure I saw Mr. Rat dragging something orange away."

"That rodent is a rogue," cried Rosie. "And he'd better return my rose right away."

"It must be rough being a rat," remarked Robert. "Rats live in very dreary places."

"Really?" said Rosie.

"It *is* dark and grungy down there," she agreed.
"But Mr. Rat has put my orange rose in a jar. His room
looks brighter already." Rosie thought hard.

"All right, Mr. Rat," she called. "My orange rose is
yours. The perfume will make your room smell fresh."

"Now I've only got three roses tied with a rainbow ribbon for Aunt Ruth," fretted Rosie.

Robert rumpled Rosie's hair.

"Come on, let's run after dragonflies," he said.
Rosie and Robert ran through the grass.
"I love the way dragonflies dart around," she cried.

Suddenly Rosie groaned.

"This is crazy," she said. "My purple rose has disappeared."

"Don't cry," said Robert. "I think you dropped your rose by that rock. I saw Mr. Rabbit rush into his warren with something purple."

"Mr. Rabbit's a rapscallion," protested Rosie. "He'd better return my rose right away."

"There's a terrible racket coming from down Mr. Rabbit's hole," remarked Robert.

"Really?" said Rosie.

"Rowdy rabbit children are romping everywhere," she reported.

"Mrs. Rabbit looks frazzled. But Mr. Rabbit is presenting her with my rose." Rosie thought hard.

"All right, Mr. Rabbit," she called. "My purple rose is yours, to help Mrs. Rabbit relax."

"Now I've only got two roses tied with a rainbow ribbon for Aunt Ruth's present," said Rosie.

"Do stop worrying, and I'll race you to that redbud tree," replied Robert.

"Right!" called Rosie, and off she ran.

Suddenly Rosie rubbed her eyes.

"This is ridiculous," she wailed. "My red rose has disappeared."

"Dry your tears, Rosie," said Robert. "I think you dropped your rose near the roots of the tree. I saw Mrs. Robin carry something red up to her nest."

"Mrs. Robin's a rascal," roared Rosie. "She'd better return my rose right away."

"I heard a rumor that Mr. Robin has raging strep throat," said Robert. "He's had to resign from the bird chorus."

"Really?" said Rosie.

"Mr. Robin has a scarf around his throat," she declared. "Mrs. Robin is nursing him with raspberry syrup." Rosie thought hard.

"All right, Mrs. Robin," she called. "My red rose is yours. It will cheer up Mr. Robin. I hope his raspy throat recovers soon."

"Now I've only got one rose tied with a rainbow ribbon for Aunt Ruth's present," said Rosie.

"Poor Rosie," said Robert. "Stop fretting, and I'll teach you to turn cartwheels."

"Let me try," cried Rosie.

"Bravo!" called Robert. "You're a razzle-dazzle cartwheel star!"

"Really?" panted Rosie.

"Robert," whispered Rosie. "There's a squirrel bride sitting in the ragweed over there, and she's crying."

"I'm marrying my truelove this morning," sobbed the squirrel bride. "But I forgot to make a garland for my hair."

Rosie thought hard.

"Let's use strands of grass and my cream rose, Miss Squirrel," she said. "They'll make a pretty garland together."

"Now I've only got a rainbow ribbon to give Aunt Ruth," said Rosie.

"Aunt Ruth will adore your rainbow ribbon," reassured Robert as Rosie rang the doorbell.

"Aunt Ruth," cried Rosie. "I had four roses for your birthday. But Mr. Rat, Mr. Rabbit, Mrs. Robin, and Miss Squirrel needed them. Now I've only got a rainbow ribbon for you."

"Rosie, I already have a rose," responded Aunt Ruth. "Where is it, Aunt Ruth?" asked Rosie in surprise. "Right in front of me," said Aunt Ruth. "You're my prize rose, Rosie."

"Oh!" said Rosie. "Really?"

"Really," said Aunt Ruth.